Karen's Tuba

Look for these
and other books about Karen
in the
Baby-sitters Little Sister series:

Little Sister

Karen's Tuba

Ann M. Martin

Illustrations by Susan Tang

A
LITTLE APPLE
PAPERBACK

SCHOLASTIC INC.
New York Toronto London Auckland Sydney

ISBN 0-590-45653-9

12 11 10 9 8 7 6 5 4 3 2   3 4 5 6 7 8/9

Printed in the U.S.A.   40

First Scholastic printing, April 1993

For Eleanor Martin,
who can read the books about Karen now

Ms. Colman's First Surprise

I looked around the table at the six people who were eating dinner at my house. At one end of the table sat Mommy. At the other end sat Seth. Seth is my stepfather. Across the table sat Ms. Colman and Mr. Simmons. Next to me sat my little brother Andrew. Andrew is four going on five.

I was the sixth person at the table. I am Karen Brewer. I am seven years old. I wear glasses. I have freckles and blonde hair and blue eyes. This is my nickname: Blarin'

Karen. The kids in my class say I have a big mouth.

Guess who Ms. Colman is. She is my teacher. I felt very lucky that my teacher was eating Saturday dinner at my house. Now guess who Mr. Simmons is. Mr. Simmons is Mr. *Henry* Simmons, Ms. Colman's fiancé. He and Ms. Colman are going to get married.

I got married once. It happened on the playground at school. I married Ricky Torres. Ricky is in my class at school. (He wears glasses, too.) Of course, Ricky and I are just pretend married. But Ms. Colman and Mr. Simmons are going to get married for real.

Ms. Colman was talking to Mommy about the wedding gown she was going to wear.

"I would like lace and seed pearls on the front," she was saying.

Andrew nudged me. "She wants *seeds* on her wedding dress?"

I sighed. Andrew has so much to learn.

"Not seeds, seed *pearls*," I whispered to him. "They are very pretty little pearls. Mommy has some on a necklace. I will show them to you after dinner."

"Okay." Andrew arranged his peas in a nice design around the tomatoes from his salad. He yawned. I could tell he was bored.

But not me. I love hearing about weddings. And I had heard quite a lot about Ms. Colman's wedding plans. My teacher was getting to be good friends with Mommy and Seth. They were always eating dinner together. This was the second time that Mr. Simmons had come over for dinner, too. None of the other kids in my class spent as much time with Ms. Colman (or Mr. Simmons) as I did. I felt sort of sorry for them. We all just love Ms. Colman.

"I wish," Ms. Colman was saying, "that my relatives did not live so far away. Did I tell you that my sister might not even be able to come to the wedding? She and her family live in Oregon."

"What about the rest of your family?" asked Seth.

"My mother lives in Chicago. I do not have much other family," replied Ms. Colman. She looked a little sad.

"I do not have much family either," said Mr. Simmons.

"It will be a very small wedding," added Ms. Colman. "Just friends."

Mommy looked across the table at my stepfather. Then she smiled at our guests. "Jean, Henry," said Mommy. (Adults get to call each other by their first names.) "I have an idea. How about if Seth and I throw a party for you before the wedding? You could give us a list of people to invite. We would really like to do that. It would be our present to you."

"Well," said Ms. Colman and Mr. Simmons. Then they smiled, too. "We accept!" said my teacher. The adults began talking and laughing.

Soon dinner was over. Ms. Colman and

Mr. Simmons had to leave. Seth handed their coats to them.

"Thank you so much," said Ms. Colman to Mommy and Seth. "It was a wonderful evening."

Then she turned to me. "I will see you in school on Monday, Karen. Oh, and look forward to a surprise."

Ms. Colman would not tell me what the surprise was, even though I guessed and guessed. So I called my sister at the big house. I had to talk to her.

News Flash!

"**K**risty!" I exclaimed when my sister answered the phone. "News flash! Ms. Colman came over for dinner, and she told me to look forward to a surprise in school on Monday."

"Cool," said Kristy. "I cannot wait to find out what it is."

Kristy is not really my sister. She is my big *step*sister. (But mostly I think of her as my sister.) Anyway, that is why Kristy lives at another house, the big house.

My family is a little bit hard to describe,

but I will try to explain it to you. A long time ago, the people in my family were Mommy and Daddy, Andrew and me. We lived together at the big house, where Kristy lives now. But after awhile, Mommy and Daddy decided they did not love each other anymore. They loved Andrew and me very much, but they did not want to live together. So they got divorced. Mommy moved out of the big house and into a little house. Andrew and I moved with her. Daddy stayed in the big house. (He grew up there.) Both of the houses are in Stoneybrook, Connecticut.

Then a surprising thing happened. Mommy and Daddy decided to get married again — but not to each other. Mommy married Seth, and Daddy married Elizabeth. And that is how Andrew and I ended up with two families, one at the big house, one at the little house. We live at the big house every other weekend and on some holidays and vacations. We live at the little house the rest of the time.

Here is who else lives at the little house: Mommy, Seth, me, Rocky, Midgie, and Emily Junior. Rocky and Midgie are Seth's cat and dog. Emily Junior is my pet rat.

Here is who lives at the big house: Daddy, Elizabeth, Kristy, Sam, Charlie, David Michael, Emily Michelle, Nannie, Andrew, me, Boo-Boo, Shannon, Goldfishie, and Crystal Light the Second. (It is a good thing the big house is so big.) Elizabeth is my stepmother. Kristy, Sam, Charlie, and David Michael are her kids, so they are my stepsister and stepbrothers. Emily Michelle is my adopted sister. She is two and a half. Daddy and Elizabeth adopted her from a faraway country called Vietnam. Nannie is Elizabeth's mother. That makes her my stepgrandmother. She helps to take care of Emily. Shannon is David Michael's puppy, Boo-Boo is Daddy's mean old tomcat, and Goldfishie and Crystal Light the Second are goldfish. (Duh.) They belong to Andrew and me.

I have a special nickname for my brother and me. The kids at school call me Blarin' Karen, but I call myself Karen Two-Two. I call my brother Andrew Two-Two. That is because we have two of so many things. (I got the idea for the name when Ms. Colman read our class a book called *Jacob Two-Two Meets the Hooded Fang*.) Andrew and I have two families and two houses, two daddies and two mommies, two cats and two dogs. I have two bicycles, one at each house. And Andrew has two tricycles. In fact, we have toys and books and clothes at *both* houses. That is so we do not have to pack much when we go from the little house to the big house, or from the big house to the little house. I even have two best friends, Hannie Papadakis and Nancy Dawes. Hannie lives across from the big house. Nancy lives next to the little house. But we are always together at school. That is because we are in Ms. Colman's second-grade class. Hannie and Nancy and I are such good friends we call ourselves the Three Musketeers.

"I wonder," I said to Kristy, "if Ms. Colman's surprise is an animal. Maybe we are going to get a pet to keep Hootie company." (Hootie is our class guinea pig.)

"Maybe," replied Kristy. "You will just have to wait and see."

3

Violas and Violins

Wait.

That is not one of my favorite words. Sometimes I wish no one had ever thought of it. I hate waiting. But when I arrived at school on Monday, I found out I had to wait for the surprise.

"Ms. Colman!" I exclaimed as soon as she came into the room. "What is the surprise? Will you tell us now?"

Ms. Colman smiled and shook her head. "I am sorry, but you will have to wait until after lunch and recess for the surprise."

"What surprise? What surprise?" My classmates crowded around Ms. Colman's desk. They all talked at once.

This is who was in that crowd: Ricky Torres, my husband. Natalie Springer. (She wears glasses, like Ricky and me. Ms. Colman makes us glasses-wearers sit in the front row so we can see the blackboard better.) Hannie and Nancy. (They get to sit together in the back row. I wish I could sit with them like I did before I needed glasses.) Pamela Harding, who is my best enemy. She thinks she is so great. Jannie and Leslie, who are Pamela's good friends. Addie Sidney, who uses a wheelchair because she has cerebral palsy. Bobby Gianelli and Hank Reubens, who are Ricky's friends. (Bobby is a bully.) Terri and Tammy, who are twins. And some other kids. I have an interesting class.

"You will find out about the surprise this afternoon," Ms. Colman told us again. So there was nothing to do but W-A-I-T.

* * *

When recess was over, my friends and I hurried into our classroom. We sat quietly in our seats. We were ready for the surprise.

"Boys and girls," said Ms. Colman, "I would like to introduce you to Mrs. Dade." She looked at the door. A young teacher walked into our room. I had seen her around school, but I had not known her name. "Mrs. Dade teaches instrumental music," explained Ms. Colman.

Ms. Colman sat down at her desk, and Mrs. Dade took her place in front of the classroom. "Hi," she said. "I am glad to meet you. I see some familiar faces here." She smiled at us. Then she disappeared into the hallway. When she entered the room again, she was pushing a cart. And on the cart were a violin, a flute, a trumpet, and some other musical instruments. (I did not know their names.)

"Class," said Mrs. Dade, "we are going to begin a special unit in music. Each of you is going to learn to play an instrument."

"Just us?" I asked. (I remembered to raise my hand first.)

"All the second-graders," replied Mrs. Dade. "Your class will also learn how to play together as a band," she went on. "Now, you will be able to choose from these instruments — and more. Some other instruments are down the hall in the band room. I could not bring them all with me." Mrs. Dade showed us a trombone, a viola, a saxophone, and a clarinet.

I could not believe it. I was going to learn to play music. I was going to play in a band. What a gigundoly wonderful surprise!

Mrs. Dade put the instruments back on the cart. Then she handed out permission slips. "Remember to ask an adult to sign your slip," she said. "You will need to be able to bring your instrument home to practice. On Mondays and Wednesdays I will be giving each of you a lesson on the instrument you choose. On Fridays I will teach you together. I will teach you how to play as a band. Bring your signed slips to

14

school on Wednesday. You may choose your instruments then."

My friends and I crowded around the cart. Hannie said she wanted to play the violin. Nancy wanted to play the clarinet. And I wanted to play the flute. But first I would have to W-A-I-T for Wednesday.

Hatey Hoffman

On Tuesday my classmates and I had another surprise. But it was not as good as the one we had had on Monday.

Ms. Colman did not come to school. She was absent. So a substitute teacher took her place.

The substitute had taught us before. Once, she taught us for an entire month. That was when Ms. Colman was sick in the hospital. The substitute's name is Mrs. Hoffman, but guess what I called her at first. I called her Hatey Hoffman. That was

17

because my friends and I thought she was mean. Mean and strict. But we just needed to learn to get along with each other. After that happened, we liked Hatey and Hatey liked us. I stopped calling her Hatey and started calling her Mrs. Hoffman. When Ms. Colman came back to school we gave Mrs. Hoffman a good-bye party. We knew we would miss her.

So I was pretty happy to see Mrs. Hoffman that Tuesday morning. But I was worried about Ms. Colman.

"Where is she?" I asked Mrs. Hoffman nervously.

"Just home with a cold, Karen," she answered. "She will be back tomorrow."

"Are you sure?"

"Pretty sure. This time tomorrow, you will be talking to Ms. Colman."

"Okay," I said. I felt better.

After lunch, the Three Musketeers ran onto the playground.

"What should we do today?" I asked.

18

"Monkey bars!" said Nancy. But the monkey bars were too crowded.

"Swings!" said Hannie. But only one swing was empty. We needed three. All next to each other.

"Hopscotch!" I said. But Pamela and her friends beat us to the last court. We could not find chalk to draw another.

So we linked our arms together and walked around the playground.

"Big-kid alert! Big-kid alert!" cried Nancy when we walked too close to some fourth-grade girls.

We started to steer around them. But I heard one of the girls say, ". . . and she never came back."

"Shh!" I hissed to Hannie and Nancy. "Listen."

We walked behind the girls for a few moments.

"What is it?" asked Hannie.

I pulled Hannie and Nancy to the kindergartners' sandbox, and we sat down on the edge. "They were talking about a

teacher. One of their old teachers," I told my friends. "They said she left school to get married and she never came back."

"Never came back!" repeated Hannie and Nancy. They gasped.

I nodded my head seriously. "She decided she wanted to have children and work at home. So she did."

"Would Ms. Colman do that?" asked Nancy.

"She said she wouldn't. We already asked her," replied Hannie. "Remember?"

"What if she changes her mind?" I said. "Maybe that other teacher planned to come back, but the wedding made her change her mind."

"Well, what would we do without Ms. Colman?" asked Hannie.

"We would have a substitute forever," replied Nancy.

"Maybe the substitute would be Mrs. Hoffman," I said. "That would not be so bad. It would not be great, but it would not be bad."

"Better than someone we do not know," added Nancy.

I sighed. I tried to think of happier things, like the band.

Karen's Mistake

The next day was Wednesday, and Ms. Colman was back. Just as Mrs. Hoffman had said she would be.

"How are you feeling?" I asked her.

"Much better, thank you," answered Ms. Colman. And then she sneezed, but only once. And she had not stuffed any Kleenex up her sleeve, so I decided she was okay.

When recess was over that day, my classmates and I ran to our desks and sat down quietly. We could not wait for Mrs. Dade.

It was time to choose our instruments. I was still hoping for a flute.

"Good afternoon, class," said Mrs. Dade a few minutes later. She had poked her head around the doorway. "Will you please follow me to the music room?"

My friends and I lined up and walked down the hallway to the music room. It looked like most of the other rooms in our school, except that there were no desks. Only chairs. And the chairs were kind of jumbled up. They were not in rows.

And, of course, there were the instruments. All of them. More than Mrs. Dade had brought to our class on Monday. They were lined up across the front of the room, under the blackboard. A parade of instruments. Saxophones and violins and clarinets and a tuba and a cello and some flutes and more. One or two or three of each. Enough for every student in both of the second-grade classes.

"Please sit down," said Mrs. Dade.

Hannie and Nancy and our friends and I sat in the jumbly chairs. I kept looking at the flutes. I stared at them until I heard a sound. Paper rustling. Rustling everywhere. I looked around. The other kids were reaching into their pockets or purses or book bags, pulling out papers, and unfolding them. What were —

Uh-oh. I knew what those papers were. They were the permission slips. We were supposed to hand them to Mrs. Dade today, so she could give us our instruments. And I had forgotten to bring mine to school. I had also forgotten to ask Mommy or Seth to sign it. That permission slip was lying on the table in my room where I had left it on Monday. And it was still blank. What a mistake.

"Nancy," I whispered, nudging her. "I forgot my slip."

"Oops," said Nancy. "Well, maybe it will not matter."

But it did.

I raised my hand. "Mrs. Dade?" I said. "I forgot my permission slip. May I still get my instrument today?"

"Oh, Karen," said Mrs. Dade. She sounded sad, or maybe disappointed. But not angry. "I am sorry. I cannot let you have an instrument until I know it is all right for you to take it home."

"It is okay," I told her.

"I need to hear that from an adult," said Mrs. Dade gently.

"All right. I will bring the slip on Friday then," I said. "I will give it to you at our next class. I promise."

"Okay," said Mrs. Dade. "But Karen, I am afraid you will not be able to choose from many instruments. The rest of the second-graders will have taken theirs home by then. Only a few will be left."

I sighed. Then I watched my classmates choose their instruments. Hannie got a violin, and Nancy got a clarinet. Just what they had hoped for. By the time music class was over, a lot of instruments were still parading across the front of the room. Including one flute. I hoped it would be there for me on Friday.

Karen's Tuba

"Mrs. Dade! Oh, Mrs. Dade!" I called. "I remembered my permission slip!"

It was Friday afternoon. Recess was over. My friends and I were ready for music class. Mrs. Dade had just walked into our room.

"Indoor voice, Karen," Ms. Colman reminded me.

"Oops. Sorry," I said. Sometimes I get a little too excited. Then I use my noisy outdoor voice when I am inside and should be using my quiet indoor voice. Adults are always reminding me to settle down.

Mrs. Dade smiled at me. "Good for you for remembering that slip," she said. "In a few minutes you can see what is left in the music room." Mrs. Dade paused. Then she added, "I am afraid it is not much."

Well, if that flute was there I would be fine.

Mrs. Dade led our class down the hall. My friends were carrying their instruments. They were all talking about them. They had had two whole days to try to play them.

"My violin sounds like this," said Hannie. "Skreek, skreek, skreek."

I giggled.

"The trombone is hard to play," said Ricky. "I have not hit a good note yet. My cousin said I sound like a sick goose."

I giggled again.

"Well, my flute sounds perfectly lovely," said Pamela. "Like an angel singing."

No one paid attention to her.

When we reached the music room I

looked for the row of instruments under the blackboard. All I saw were chairs. And a tuba in the corner.

"Well, what's left?" I asked Mrs. Dade.

She pointed to the tuba.

"That's *it*? Where's the flute? I thought the flute would be here."

"Someone in the other second-grade class chose it," said Mrs. Dade.

"You mean I have to play the *tuba*?" I exclaimed.

"Well — " Mrs. Dade began to say.

But I could not hear the rest of her sentence. My classmates were giggling and whispering and talking to each other.

"Karen, the tuba is perfect for you!" cried Pamela.

"For you and your big mouth," added Bully Bobby.

"Blarin' Karen, Blarin' Karen," Leslie chanted.

Mrs. Dade clapped her hands. "Boys and girls!" she said loudly. "That is enough. I

30

do not want to hear another word about Karen and the tuba. If I do, you may go right back to your classroom."

After that, no one *said* anything about me and my tuba. But they still giggled and snickered behind their hands.

"Karen," said Mrs. Dade. "You may come get your tuba."

I stood up. Next to me, Ricky was turning red from trying not to laugh. Behind me, Pamela was holding up a sheet of paper. She was laughing into it. Addie had bent over so she was resting her head and arms on the tray of her wheelchair. Her shoulders shook as she giggled. Even Hannie and Nancy looked as if they were hiding smiles.

I ignored everybody. I let Mrs. Dade hand me the tuba. (It weighed a ton.) Then I sat down again. Music class began.

I had a talk with myself. This is what I said: "Karen, you have to play the tuba. No other instrument is left. And you want to play in the band. So you might as well make the best of things." (I knew Daddy would have said that to me.) Then I told myself, "And if you have to play the tuba, you might as well be good at it."

Okay. I will show everyone, I decided. I will become a great tuba player.

Karen's Duet

That afternoon I lugged my tuba home from school. Mrs. Dawes picked up Nancy and me in her car.

"Goodness, Karen," she said. "That tuba is almost as big as you are."

"I know." I struggled through the back door. Danny was asleep in his car seat. There was just barely enough room for Danny, the tuba, and me. "But I am going to become a great tuba player," I told Mrs. Dawes.

"Good for you," she replied.

* * *

My tuba took another car ride that day. Before supper, Mommy drove Andrew and me to Daddy's house for the weekend. I brought the tuba with me.

When we first arrived at the big house, Andrew and I were very busy. Everyone was there to greet us. We talked and talked, and I showed off the tuba. Then it was dinnertime. After that, Daddy and Elizabeth took us out for ice cream. Finally, when we came home, I carried the tuba to my room. I took it out of its case.

"Okay, tuba," I said to it. "I hope you sound pretty."

It was the very first time I had tried to play my tuba. In music class, Mrs. Dade had talked to us about notes and how to read them. (Musical notes, not notes you pass in class.) We had not even touched our instruments. Now I held the tuba to my mouth.

I blew hard.

HONK!

"Yikes!" I shrieked.

I tried again. *Honk, honk, honk.*

A few minutes later, Sam came into my room. "How's it going?" he asked.

"Fine. I guess."

Sam reminded me that he has played in the band at his high school. And he has tried more than one instrument. "Maybe I could help you," he added. "Do you need some tips?"

"I'll say," I replied. "I have not had one single lesson. All I can do is this." I honked a few more times.

"Well, that is a start," said Sam. Then he sat down next to me. And that is how Sam gave me my first tuba lesson ever.

"Thank you very much," I told him. "I plan to become a world-famous tuba player one day. The best tuba player of all time."

"Good luck," replied Sam.

On Saturday, Hannie came over. She brought along her violin.

"Let's play a duet," I said to her.

"But we do not know how to play anything yet," said Hannie.

"Let's just try. We have to start somewhere."

"Okay." Hannie held the violin to her chin. She touched the bow to it.

Skreek.

I honked away on the tuba.

A few minutes later Sam came into my room. He listened to the honking and skreeking. "How about a lesson?" Sam asked Hannie.

Sam gave her a lesson. Then he left us alone. Hannie and I pretended we were famous musicians. We played and played. But when we went downstairs later, I noticed that Nannie was wearing earmuffs. And Shannon and Boo-Boo were hiding in the laundry room.

Oh, well. At least nobody at the big house had called me Blarin' Karen. I was excited about my lesson on Monday with Mrs. Dade. So what if I could not play the flute? The tuba was fine with me.

Practice Makes Perfect

On Sunday evening, my tuba and I went back to the little house. On Monday we went to school together. Soon I would have my first lesson with Mrs. Dade. I could not wait to show her what Sam had taught me.

All morning, kids kept leaving Ms. Colman's room to go see Mrs. Dade. First Addie and Hank left for their saxophone lesson. Then Hannie and Leslie and Natalie left for their violin lesson.

I sat at my desk and W-A-I-T-E-D.

Finally Ms. Colman called my name.

"You may go to the music room now," she added. "Have fun."

I stood up. I picked up my tuba. I think one person giggled at me, but that was all. (It was probably Pamela.)

I had to walk to Mrs. Dade's room all alone, since nobody else was playing the tuba. I told myself I was very special, because I would be able to have a *private* lesson.

"Hello, Karen," Mrs. Dade greeted me. "Are you ready for your first lesson?"

I sat in a chair across from Mrs. Dade. "I am ready for my *second* lesson," I replied. "My big brother Sam gave me a lesson on Friday night. Sam has played in the band in high school. He sort of knows how to play three instruments," I told her proudly.

"Does he? Well, let me see what you can do."

I honked on the tuba. I blew a little harder than I had meant to. Mrs. Dade jumped.

"My goodness," she said. "Well, I see

Sam taught you how to hold the tuba properly. That is very good."

"Yes," I replied. "Thank you. He showed me where my fingers go."

Mrs. Dade and I worked hard during the lesson. Mrs. Dade was patient. I tried to follow her instructions. But by the time the lesson was over, I could still only *HONK*!

"Karen," said Mrs. Dade. "Maybe you would like to play percussion instead. The tuba is a difficult instrument. I am sure I could find a triangle and a tambourine and some castanets for you."

"No, thank you," I replied. I knew those were for kindergartners.

Mrs. Dade sighed. "All right. You must practice twenty minutes a day on your tuba."

Twenty minutes? Was that all? "I will practice for an hour," I told my teacher. "Practice makes perfect."

Karen's Concert

Maybe the tuba was a difficult instrument, but there was one good thing about it. It was *my* instrument. I could not believe Mrs. Dade had tried to talk me into playing the triangle and the tambourine. *Any*one could play those. But not just anyone could play the tuba. And I *had* planned to prove I could play well. (Well enough to travel around the world giving concerts.)

That was why I decided to practice an hour each day. It was really the only way to become famous.

* * *

By Friday, I had had another private lesson with Mrs. Dade. And I had practiced for four hours at the little house. I could play a few different notes. They were the notes I needed for "Mary Had a Little Lamb" and the first part of "Jingle Bells." Everyone else in my class was learning those notes and those songs on their instruments.

After recess, my friends and I carried our violins and clarinets and saxophones and trombones to the music room. The chairs there were arranged in two semicircles, one inside the other. Mrs. Dade showed us where to sit.

"Now," she said. "Are you ready to be a real band?"

"Yes!" we cried.

"All right. Let's begin with the first line of 'Mary Had a Little Lamb.'"

Honk! Skreet! Hoot! Baroo!

We sounded horrible! We sounded like a car accident. I did not understand. How

had that happened? We had been practicing for four days.

"Let's try that again," said Mrs. Dade patiently.

Honk! Skreek! Hoot! Baroo!

I raised my hand.

"Yes, Karen?"

"Mrs. Dade, we sound awful." I glanced around at my friends' faces. They looked as disappointed as I felt.

"Don't worry," said Mrs. Dade. "Almost every class starts out just like this. In a few weeks, you will be surprised at how good you sound. I promise. In fact, I have so much faith in you that I am planning for you and the other second-graders to put on a concert at school when your band unit is over."

A *con*cert? No way. Usually, I just adore performing for an audience. But not with this band. We would never be ready for a concert. Our parents and brothers and sisters would come to hear us, and they would just laugh. Maybe they would even leave before the concert was over.

Already, the big kids at school were laughing at us second-graders. I heard them talking about our music lessons. They said they had to wear earplugs when they passed Mrs. Dade's room.

I was not the only one who was worried about the concert.

When the bell rang at the end of the day, my friends and I were quiet. We stood up slowly. We put on our coats slowly.

"We are going to make fools of ourselves," Ricky said to me.

"I hope people will not have to *pay* to hear us," said Addie. "That concert will not be worth one penny."

Well, I was worried, too. But Mrs. Dade had said we were going to put on a concert. So I decided we better make the best of it. It was just like playing my tuba. At least we ought to *try* to do well. We should work hard.

I told my friends so.

"We can do it, you know," I said to everybody. "We can put on a great concert. We will just have to practice extra hard."

I was not sure anyone believed me. I was not even sure I believed myself.

A Surprise for
Ms. Colman

"Come on, you guys," I said to Hannie and Nancy. "Let's go."

The Three Musketeers walked slowly out of school. We did not even hurry up when we saw Mommy's car.

Andrew waved to my friends and me from the backseat. "Hey, Hannie!" he called. "How come you're riding with us today?"

"Hannie is coming over to play," I told him.

"Aren't you happy about that?" he asked me.

"Yes, but we have a big problem. You are too little to understand it, though."

"I am not too little!" cried Andrew.

"Okay. Settle down," said Mommy.

Nancy and Hannie and I were very quiet as we rode home. When we reached the little house, we ran straight to my room.

"We better practice," I said.

We sat on my bed in a row. I was holding my tuba, Nancy was holding her clarinet, Hannie was holding her violin.

"Okay," said Nancy. " 'Mary Had a Little Lamb.' And a-one and a-two and a-three and a-four and a-five. Hey, come on, you guys. We are supposed to begin playing." I started to play. Then Hannie started to play. "No, I mean we are supposed to begin playing at the same time," said Nancy. "Wait. Let me try something different. Ready, set, GO!" she cried.

Mary . . . had . . . a . . . little . . . lamb. . . .

"That was not bad!" exclaimed Hannie when we had finished.

We tried the song again. Hannie was right. We did not sound *so* bad. We sounded a teeny bit better. Like a traffic jam instead of a car wreck.

We played for a little while longer. Then we laid down our instruments.

"Ms. Colman snuck down to the music room today," I said. "I saw her listening to us. She was smiling."

"I do not want Ms. Colman to get married and go away," said Nancy. She sighed. "I will miss her."

"She will probably come back," said Hannie. But she did not sound as if she believed what she had said.

"Even if she comes back, I will miss her while she is gone," said Nancy.

"Me too," I said.

"Me three," said Hannie.

"You know what?" said Nancy. "We should do something special for Ms. Colman. I mean, our class should. We should plan a surprise for her since she is getting married."

"That is a great idea!" I exclaimed. "Now let's see. What could we do?"

"We could collect money and buy her a present," said Hannie.

"We could bake her a cake," suggested Nancy. "A wedding cake."

"And give her a party," added Hannie.

"Wait!" I cried. "I know! I thought of something that will *really* surprise her. I bet we could learn how to play 'Here Comes the Bride' on our instruments. All of us. Our whole class. And we can play it at our band concert. Just for Ms. Colman."

"Won't she hear us practicing the song in the music room?" asked Nancy.

I shook my head. "Nope. We will learn to play the song in secret. We will not tell anyone about it. Not even Mrs. Dade. We can practice by ourselves at home. Boy, will everyone be surprised when we play it at the concert."

"Excellent!" exclaimed Hannie and Nancy.

That weekend the Three Musketeers called up every kid in Ms. Colman's class. We told them about our idea. We made sure to say, "Remember. It is a secret. Do not say a word to anyone."

The Secret Meeting

"Pssst. Secret meeting on the playground after lunch. Pass it along," I whispered to Natalie Springer.

Natalie pulled Tammy aside. "Psst. Secret meeting on the playground after lunch. Pass it along," she whispered.

Tammy leaned over to Terri. Terri passed the secret to Hank. Hank whispered it to Bully Bobby.

It was Monday morning. My friends and I were in our classroom. Ms. Colman had just arrived. I wanted to make sure everyone knew about the meeting. Everyone except Ms. Colman. We were going to talk about the surprise song for her.

At lunch my classmates and I ate quickly. Then we ran out of the cafeteria. We met by the monkey bars on the playground.

I took charge.

"Everyone knows about the surprise for Ms. Colman," I said. "Right?"

"Right!" cried my friends.

"SHH! Keep your voices down!" I hissed. "This is a *secret*. Now — does everyone think it is a good idea?"

"Yes," whispered my friends.

"Do you all promise to keep the secret?"

"Yes."

"Does anybody have a question?" I asked.

Natalie raised her hand. "How will we learn the song?" she wanted to know.

"Easy," I replied. "At least, I think it will be easy. I talked to my big brother Sam. I told him about our secret — "

"You *told* someone?" cried Pamela. "Already?"

"Blarin' Karen!" said Bobby gleefully.

I glared at my friends. "Do you want to make the surprise work or not?" I demanded. "We need help with it. And Sam can help us. He has played in his band at the *high* school. He knows how to play *six* instruments." That was not quite true, but I needed to make Sam sound good. "He has helped me with my tuba, and he has helped Hannie with her violin. He said he can find easy music for 'Here Comes the Bride.' He says he thinks we can all learn to play the song. So do not worry. Sam will help us read the notes."

"Just remember that we have to do our best," spoke up Nancy. "This surprise must be extra special. It is our wedding present for Ms. Colman."

"It might be our good-bye present," I added.

"What do you mean?" asked Addie. Her eyes grew wide.

I told the kids about teachers who leave and do not come back.

"But Ms. Colman *said* she was coming back," Hank pointed out.

I nodded. "I know. She says that *now*. But what if she changes her mind?"

"If Ms. Colman left, who would be our teacher?" asked Natalie. Her lip was trembling, and her eyes had filled with tears.

"Mrs. Hoffman, I hope," I replied. "But we cannot be sure."

"We *better* be sure," said Ricky. "I don't want some substitute we never met before to come in and take Ms. Colman's place."

Natalie's lip stopped quivering. She wiped her eyes. Then she looked at me. "We could make an invitation for Mrs. Hoffman," she said. "We could invite her to be our permanent teacher after Ms. Colman leaves. I bet she would not turn down a nice invitation."

So we decided to form an invitation committee. These were the people on the committee: the Three Musketeers, Natalie, Ricky, and Hank.

The Boys' Wedding

The secret meeting was held on Monday. Five days went by. I had two more tuba lessons with Mrs. Dade. The band had one more lesson with her. School ended for the week. Andrew and I went to the big house. And on Saturday, the Three Musketeers gathered at Hannie's house. We were going to rehearse "Here Comes the Bride."

When I rang the bell at the Papadakises' house, Hannie answered it. She let my tuba and me inside.

"Is Nancy here yet?" I asked.

"Not yet. But she's on her way."

A few minutes later, the bell rang again.

"Nancy's here!" I cried.

The Three Musketeers charged up the stairs to Hannie's room. Hannie had set up chairs for us. "Just like in Mrs. Dade's class," she said.

We sat in the chairs. We began our secret song.

Dum, dum, da-dum. Dum, dum, da-dum. Dum, dum, da-*skreeek*.

"Start over," said Hannie.

Dum, dum, da-dum. Dum, dum, da-dum. Dum, dum, da-*honk*.

"Start over," I said.

We kept starting the song over. But every time we tried to play this one high note, somebody made a mistake.

"Start over," said Nancy. She was saying it for about the fifteenth time. But this time nobody started playing. We had heard a noise.

"What is that?" I whispered.

We peered into the hallway. There were

Linny Papadakis and David Michael. David Michael was wearing a suit and his best shoes. (They had been shined.) Linny was wearing a long white dress and a pair of white heels. He was carrying a bouquet of plastic flowers.

"What are you doing?" demanded Hannie.

"What does it look like?" replied David Michael. "We are getting married."

"I am a bride," added Linny. "And here I come." He began to sing our secret song. "Dum, dum da-dum. Here comes the bride."

"After we get married, will you quit playing?" asked David Michael. He did not wait for an answer. He turned to Linny. "Come along, my lovely wife. Let us go on our honeymoon." The boys ran away.

I looked at Nancy and Hannie. We tried to pretend we were mad at the boys. But we could not. We began to giggle. Then we put away our instruments. We needed a break from practicing.

The Missing Tuba

"Daddy, may I start practicing now?" I asked.

Daddy looked at his watch. "In another half an hour," he told me. "At nine o'clock. Everyone should be awake by then."

"What if they are not?"

"Well, they should be. You can wake them up with a beautiful tuba solo."

It was the next day, Sunday morning. Daddy and Nannie and Andrew and Emily and I had just eaten breakfast. I was ready to practice some more, but now I would have to W-A-I-T. While I W-A-I-T-E-D, I helped Daddy outside in the gardens. But only until nine o'clock. At nine, I ran inside and sat on my bed with my tuba.

I played a scale. La, la, la, la, la, la, la, la. I tried to play softly because Sam and Charlie were not awake yet. I played the scale a few more times. Then I switched to "Mary Had a Little Lamb." I played it slowly. Then I played it faster. Then I played "Here Comes the Bride."

Dum, dum, da-dum. Dum, dum, da-dum. Dum, dum, da-*honk*.

I heard a snort from down the hallway. Then Sam appeared at my door. He was wearing his pajamas. They were very wrinkled. His hair was standing on end. He did not look happy.

"Karen, do you know what time it is?" he said.

"Nine-oh-eight," I replied. "Daddy said I could start practicing at nine o'clock, so I did. Did I wake you up?"

"Yes. But I had to get up anyway." Sam

went back down the hall.

Dum, dum, da-dum. Dum, dum —

"Are you going to play that song all day?" someone asked.

I looked up. Now David Michael and Andrew were standing in my doorway.

"I am going to play it for the next month," I told them.

They stuck their tongues out at me. I stuck mine out at them. Then I practiced for an hour. Then I took a break. I took a break until lunch was over. And then I decided Hannie and I should practice together again.

I went to my room to get my tuba.

My tuba was not on my bed where I had left it. It was not anywhere.

My tuba was gone.

"Dad-dee!" I shrieked. "Elizabeth! Kristy! Nannie! Help!"

Everyone came running.

"My tuba is gone!" I wailed.

"For heaven's sake," said Daddy. "You do not need to make such a fuss."

"I thought you had hurt yourself," added Elizabeth.

"But it is *gone!*" I cried. "And Mrs. Dade said we have to take care of our instruments. We are responsible for them." I paused. "I bet David Michael took it. Or Andrew. They do not like my practicing."

"We did not take it!" replied David Michael crossly. He was standing in my doorway, too. "And to prove it, we will help you find it. Everybody, spread out and search," he ordered.

Kristy and my brothers and I looked all through the big house. First we looked downstairs. Then we climbed the steps to the second floor.

"Hey, what is that?" said David Michael. He put his hand to his ear. We stopped to listen. "Moose sounds," said David Michael. "It sounds like a moose is loose in Emily Michelle's bedroom."

Of course, no moose was in Emily's room. But my tuba was there. Emily was trying to play it. I guess she wanted a turn.

64

"Gee, Karen," said David Michael. "She plays almost as badly as you do."

I ignored my brother. I was just glad to have my tuba back. In fact, I was so glad that I gave Emily a lesson. *Honk, honk, honk.* She liked playing the tuba.

The Invitation

One day after school, the invitation committee had a meeting. We met at Nancy's house. Nancy, Hannie, Natalie, Hank, Ricky, and I sat around the Daweses' kitchen table. (Mrs. Dawes had to bring in extra chairs for us.) We drank some juice and ate some fruit.

Then I said, "Okay. It is time to get started."

"How do we start?" asked Hank.

"Mmm. We need some paper and pencils," I said.

Nancy found three pencils, and a pad of paper with wide lines.

"Perfect," I told her. "Thank you. Now we have to decide what to say to Mrs. Hoffman. Remember, we want her to like the invitation. We want her to say yes to it. This has to be just right."

"I know," said Natalie. "Start with *Dear Mrs. Hoffman, You are our favorite teacher ever. We like you —* "

"No, we cannot say that," Hannie interrupted. "Ms. Colman is our favorite teacher ever. Mrs. Hoffman is our second favorite."

"But we cannot say that, either," spoke up Ricky. "We cannot tell Mrs. Hoffman she is our *second* favorite teacher. That will hurt her feelings and then she will not want to be our teacher at all."

"Wait, wait, wait," said Nancy. "Why do we have to say who is our favorite teacher? Let's just tell Mrs. Hoffman we like her a lot, and we want her to come back and stay with us when Ms. Colman is gone. We want her for the rest of second grade."

"Excuse me," said Natalie, "but doesn't an invitation have to say what time and what day and what place?"

"If you are having a party, it does," I told her. "But this is not about a party. Now, come on, you guys."

"All right," said Hank. "Write down *Dear Mrs. Hoffman*."

I printed it carefully.

"Now," said Nancy, "write *We like you very much*."

I printed that, too. Then my friends and I wrote some other things. When we had finished, our invitation looked like this:

DEAR MRS. HOFFMAN,
WE LIKE YOU VERY MUCH. YOU ARE OUR BEST
SU~~BSTA S~~I'S SUBSTITUTE. SOON MS. COLMAN
IS GOING AWAY TO GET MARIED. SHE SAYS SHE
IS COMING BAKE. WE DO NOT THINK SO. WE
HAVE HERD ABOUT TEACHERS WHO GO AWAY AND
DO NOT COME BAKE. SO WILL YOU PLEASE BE
OUR PE~~R~~ P~~REMA~~ OUR SUBSTITUTE FOREVER?
THAT WOULD MEAN A LOT TO US.

OH BY THE WAY WE ARE GOING TO HAVE A
BAND CONSURT AT SCHOOL. WOULD YOU LIKE TO
COME? YOU COULD BE OUR SPECIAL GUESSED.

LOTS OF LOVE FROM,
MS. COLMAN's CLASS

"What should we do about the cross-
outs?" asked Natalie. She was frowning
down at the invitation.

"Someone better copy it over," said Hannie. "We do not want to send a messy invitation to Mrs. Hoffman. She might not
like it."

"I will copy it over," I said. I sighed
loudly. "And I will fix the spelling."

"And you know what? I think everyone
in our class should sign it," said Ricky.
"Then Mrs. Hoffman will know we are
serious."

"And maybe we should decorate it," said
Nancy. "I could color some flowers around
the edges."

So we set to work. Three days later, the
invitation was really and truly finished. I
mailed it myself.

Bloopers

"Secret meeting. Pass it along."

"Secret meeting. Pass it along."

My classmates and I needed another meeting on the playground. It was a Thursday. In one week and one day, the band concert was going to take place. We had to be ready with our surprise for Ms. Colman.

We held our secret meeting at the monkey bars after lunch.

"Has everyone been practicing the song?" I asked.

"Yes!"

"Has anyone *not* been practicing it?"

Nobody said a word. Was that true? Every single person in my class had been practicing the secret song? Even Bully Bobby? That was great.

"Is anyone having trouble with it?" I asked.

A few kids raised their hands.

I nodded. "We might need a little help now. Also, you know what? We need to practice together — our whole class — at least once before the concert."

"How are we going to do that?" asked Leslie.

"We will have to practice at somebody's house. Over the weekend, I guess. Maybe we can practice at my father's house. We could sit in the big backyard if the weather is nice."

Addie raised her hand. "I have a question," she said. "There is something I do not understand. For weeks we have been practicing 'Here Comes the Bride' at home. Our families have heard it over and over.

I do not think it will be a surprise to them."

"Yes, it will," I replied. "Because *they* do not know it is a surprise for Ms. *Colman*. And they do not know we taught it to ourselves. Now, everybody, tell your parents we decided we need an extra rehearsal before the concert, so we will sound our very best. I will ask Daddy if we can rehearse at my house on Saturday afternoon. Okay, this secret meeting is over. Let's go play."

And that is how my friends and I arranged for a special rehearsal of "Here Comes the Bride." By two o'clock on Saturday, every single kid in Ms. Colman's class was in my backyard. We were sitting in folding chairs. Sam was our bandleader. He said he would give us as much help as we needed. This was very nice of him.

"Okay," said Sam to my class. "Let me hear what you can do."

I lifted the tuba to my lips. Hannie raised her violin. My class began to play.

Dum, dum, da-dum. Dum, dum, da-dum. Dum, dum, da-*honk*, *skreek*, *baroo*, *eech*, *bloot*.

"Yikes!" I cried. "That was a blooper."

"I'll say," said Sam. "Try it again."

We played the song again. We sounded just the same. Another blooper.

Natalie raised her hand. "Excuse me. Sir?" she said.

"Who, me?" replied Sam. "Yes?"

"I can never play that note right, sir," said Natalie. "That high one. I always get stuck on it."

"Me, too," said a whole bunch of my classmates.

"Why don't you practice playing that one note for a while," suggested Sam. "Get used to the way it feels."

We played it over and over. (I spotted Nannie in the house. I saw her through the kitchen window. She was wearing the ear-muffs again.) But guess what. The next time we played the song, we sounded a little better. And by the end of the rehearsal, we sounded almost . . . good.

The Visitor

On Wednesday, my classmates and I were writing in our reading workbooks. The room was quiet. We were thinking hard.

My page was about silent vowels. Like the "e" at the end of "house." I was just wondering why we need to put that "e" at the end of "house," when I heard a knock at the door.

I glanced up. So did everyone else in the room.

Guess who walked through the door. Mrs. Hoffman.

I leaned over and nudged Ricky. "See?" I whispered. "Ms. Colman *isn't* coming back. Mrs. Hoffman must be here to say she liked our invitation, and she will be happy to be our new teacher."

"Girls and boys," said Ms. Colman. "Please put away your workbooks. Eyes up front. We have to discuss something."

"Told you so," I whispered to Ricky.

Ms. Colman and Mrs. Hoffman were standing side by side in front of the blackboard. Mrs. Hoffman was holding the invitation. Ms. Colman took it from her and held it up.

"Yesterday," she said, "Mrs. Hoffman called me. She told me she had received an invitation in the mail from my students. She said she wanted to talk to me about it."

I began to feel nervous. Neither Ms. Colman nor Mrs. Hoffman was smiling. Had my friends and I done something wrong? Were we in trouble?

"It is a lovely invitation," spoke up Mrs. Hoffman. "When I read it, I felt very flattered. I am happy that I am your best substitute. Also, I am very pleased to be invited to your concert on Friday. My husband and I will be delighted to attend."

So far, nobody seemed too mad. I wondered what would happen next.

"Class," said Ms. Colman. (She sounded serious.) "I need to tell you something. This is important."

"Here we go," I whispered to Ricky.

"After I get married," began Ms. Colman, "my husband and I are going on a short honeymoon. Then I absolutely, positively will return to Stoneybrook Academy and to you. I will be your teacher for all of second grade."

"Really?" I cried out.

"Really," said Ms. Colman. "Mr. Simmons and I have talked about this. Teach-

ing is my career. That is what I *do*."

"But what if you have a baby?" asked Pamela.

"If Mr. Simmons and I have a baby, we will both take some time off to be with the baby after he or she is born. Then we will return to work."

I raised my hand. "Will Mrs. Hoffman be our substitute while you are on your honeymoon?" I asked.

"Yes, she will," replied Ms. Colman. "So have fun with her then. Because after two weeks, I *will be back*. And Mrs. Hoffman will leave."

I breathed a gigundo sigh of relief. So did the other kids.

Mrs. Hoffman smiled at us. "Thanks again for the invitation," she said. "I am looking forward to being your substitute soon. And I will see you at the concert in two days."

After Mrs. Hoffman left, Ms. Colman smiled at us again. I knew she was not mad. I felt extra happy.

Butterflies

The bell rang.

School was over for the day. In fact, it was over for the week.

It was Friday afternoon. That evening we were going to have . . . our band concert.

I was a little tiny bit nervous.

"See you tonight!" I called to my friends as we ran out of school.

Here is what was going to happen at the concert. First, the other second-grade class was going to play their songs. Then some of the big kids were going to play solos.

They were the kids who were already extra good. They had been taking music lessons for a few years. Last of all, our class was going to perform. And just when everyone thought we had finished, we were going to play "Here Comes the Bride." Our surprise for Ms. Colman, our special teacher.

That afternoon, I could not settle down. As soon as Mrs. Dawes dropped me off, I ran inside. I ran to the kitchen to say hi to Mommy and Andrew. I ran to my bedroom to say hi to my rat. I ran downstairs again to ask Mommy a question. I ran over to Nancy's house. I ran back home.

"Karen," said Mommy. "You are making me dizzy. Please settle down."

I tried to. I really did. I sat at the table in the kitchen. "Let's color," I said to Andrew. I colored part of a fish. Then I leaped up. "All finished!" I cried.

"*I'm* not," said Andrew.

"Why don't you set the table for supper, Karen?" suggested Mommy.

I set the table too fast. I broke a plate.

"How about practicing the tuba?" said Mommy.

Honk, honk, honk. I sounded like I had not had a single lesson.

Finally Seth came home. We sat down to an early dinner. Mrs. Dade had said to be back at school by seven o'clock.

I ate one bite of baked potato. Then I jumped up. "Done!" I announced.

"Karen," said Mommy. "You only ate one bite."

And Seth added, "That is not how we excuse ourselves from the table."

I sat down again. I ate two more bites. Then I said politely, "May I please be excused?" When Mommy and Seth said yes, I ran to my room. It was time to get dressed for the concert.

I had already decided what I was going to wear. I had a new sweater that looked like an Easter egg. I put it on with a pair of stretchy black pants and my fancy black shoes. The shoes are *slip*-ons. They do not need a strap to stay on your feet. When I was dressed, I brushed my hair and tied a green ribbon in it.

I was ready for the concert.

Mommy drove Andrew and Seth and my tuba and me to school. Guess who we saw walking into school. Daddy and Elizabeth and my big-house family.

"Hi, everybody! Hi, Kristy!" I called. I ran to my sister. Then I whispered, "Did you bring the flowers?" I had given Kristy an important secret job.

"They are in my bag," Kristy whispered back. She pointed to the tote bag she was carrying.

"Oh, thank you!" I said. "Do you know what to do?"

"Yup. We will be sitting near the front."

"Okay. See you later."

It was time to find my classmates. While Mommy and I looked for them, I worried. I worried that my friends and I would make bloopers. I worried about our surprise. I worried that people would laugh at us. Worry, worry, worry.

Here Comes the Bride

The concert had begun. The other second-graders were playing. Since my classmates and I would not have to perform for awhile, we were sitting with the audience. We were sitting in the first row of seats so we could sneak backstage quickly.

My big-house family and my little-house family were sitting right behind me. Every now and then, I turned around to smile at Kristy.

My friends and I listened to the other class. They played very well. They did make some mistakes, but no one laughed at them. Then the big kids began to play. Before they finished, Ms. Colman signaled to us. Very quietly she led us out of the auditorium. Then she led us to the music room.

"Please get your instruments quietly," she whispered.

We found our instruments. Then Ms. Colman showed us onto the stage. The curtain was down. On the other side of the curtain, a fifth-grader was playing a violin solo. I saw that the chairs from Mrs. Dade's room had been set up in the two semicircles.

"Okay, find your places," whispered Ms. Colman. We sat down just as the violin stopped playing. "Now," Ms. Colman continued, "when the curtain goes up, you will be onstage. Good luck."

I glanced at Nancy and tried to smile at her, but the smile came out all wavery.

The curtain rose.

My heart beat fast in my chest. I looked

into the audience. I saw everyone from my little-house family and everyone from my big-house family. I waved to them. Some of them waved back. And they all smiled. I did not feel nervous anymore.

I watched Mrs. Dade.

My classmates and I began to play "Mary Had a Little Lamb." Once, I heard Pamela's flute make a *shneep*. But no one laughed. We finished the song. We began "Jingle Bells." Hannie lost her place and missed a few notes. My tuba went *honk*, and somebody's trumpet went *blort*. Still nobody laughed.

When we had played our last song, the audience clapped for us. I grinned.

Mrs. Dade turned around and faced the audience. It was time for her to thank everyone for coming. So I nudged Ricky.

Ricky jumped up. He dashed over to Mrs. Dade. "Excuse me," he said to the audience in a big voice. "Our class has a surprise. It is for our teacher, Ms. Colman. She is getting married soon."

Mrs. Dade looked fairly surprised herself, but she did not say anything. She watched Ricky as he returned to his seat. When he nodded to us, my friends and I began to play "Here Comes the Bride." Dum, dum, da-dum. Dum, dum, da-dum. Dum, dum, da-dum, dum, da-dum, dum, da-dum.

The audience clapped again. Ms. Colman was sitting in the front with Mr. Simmons and Mrs. Hoffman. Her eyes had filled with tears. But she was clapping. So was Mrs. Dade, whose mouth was hanging open. "How did you learn that?" she said. But I knew she did not really expect an answer. Not just then.

It was my turn to stand up. I dashed to the edge of the stage. "Kristy!" I called. Kristy ran to me with the flowers. I took them from her and waited for the audience to stop clapping. When the room was quiet, I said, "Ms. Colman, these are for you."

Ms. Colman walked onto the stage and took the flowers. "Thank you very, very much," she said.

That reminded me of something. "I have one more announcement," I said to the audience. "I want to thank my brother Sam Thomas. He helped us with the surprise. We could not have done it without him."

Sam and I smiled at each other.

Ms. Colman's
Second Surprise

The audience clapped for a long time. They liked the music they had heard at the concert. They liked our surprise. We had made a few bloopers, but no bad ones. And we had played "Here Comes the Bride" perfectly. Best of all, no one had laughed at me and my tuba. And no one had called me Blarin' Karen. I felt gigundoly happy.

The people in the audience began to stand up and put on their coats. Most of them were going home. But some of them were going to a party in Ms. Colman's room. The parents and grandparents and brothers and sisters of my classmates and me had been invited.

Ms. Colman and Mrs. Dade were standing on the stage. They could not stop asking questions.

"Did you know about the song?" Ms. Colman asked Mrs. Dade.

"Who taught you to play it?" Mrs. Dade asked my friends and me.

"When did you rehearse it?" Ms. Colman wanted to know.

My friends and I tried to answer them. Everyone was talking at once.

We were still talking as we carried our instruments off the stage, down the hall, and into our classroom.

I took a look around the room. Our guests were there — the people in my two families, Mrs. Hoffman, someone who was probably Mr. Hoffman, Mr. Henry Simmons, and a lot of other people. Ms. Colman's books had been cleared off of her desk. In their place were bottles of juice and seltzer and soda, two plates of cookies, a plate of brownies, and three bowls of potato chips. It was party time!

"Yippee!" I cried. (No one told me to use my indoor voice.) I ran to Mr. Henry Simmons. "Hi! Did you like the surprise?" I cried.

Mr. Simmons smiled. "Very much, Karen," he answered. "I liked the rest of the concert, too. You should all be proud of yourselves."

"Thank you," I said politely.

After that I just ran around for awhile. I ran to Nannie and hugged her. I ran to Sam and thanked him again. I ran to Kristy and thanked her for the flowers again. I showed off Emily Michelle to anyone who had not met her. (I made sure to tell them I had named my rat after her.) I was about to let Hootie out of the guinea pig cage when someone tapped me on the shoulder. It was Daddy.

"Karen, you need to settle down," he whispered. "And please put Hootie back."

I closed the door to Hootie's cage. I stood up. Maybe some cookies and brownies would settle me down. I reached for a handful. And Ms. Colman stepped to the front of the room.

"Class," she said. "Guests, I have an announcement to make." (Everyone stopped talking and eating and moving around. We stood still and listened.) "First," Ms. Colman continued, "I want to say congratulations to my students. Your performance was wonderful. You have worked hard and it shows. Second, I want to thank you for the surprise. Mr. Simmons and I feel very honored. And touched. And everybody, including Mrs. Dade, is impressed that you taught the song to yourselves."

"With some help from Sam," I reminded her.

"With some help from Sam," repeated Ms. Colman. "Thank you, Sam." (Sam blushed.) "The last thing I want to say," Ms. Colman went on, "involves Mr. Simmons, too." Ms. Colman reached for his

hand and they stood side by side. "Mr. Simmons and I will be getting married in one month — four weeks from tomorrow. We would like to invite all of my students and their parents to the wedding. We would like you to share the day with us."

For once, I did not know what to say. I just stared at Ms. Colman and Mr. Simmons. Then I ran to Hannie and Nancy. We jumped up and down. We giggled and screeched. We were going to the wedding!

I decided this had been one of the best nights of my life.

The Flower Girl

The concert was over. The special night was over.

Guess what else. Music class was over, too. Our band unit with Mrs. Dade had ended. Anyone who wanted more music lessons could take them privately from Mrs. Dade after school. Those kids could rent their instruments from school. The other kids had to give theirs back.

Most of us gave them back. I gave back my tuba. I had decided I did not have enough time to become a great tuba player.

But Nancy kept her clarinet and Ricky kept his trombone and, of course, Pamela kept her flute. (If you ask me, she had a long way to go before she sounded like an angel singing.)

I wondered who would be the next kid at school to play the tuba. So far, no one was using it. It just sat in the music room. Maybe I would be the only second-grader in the history of Stoneybrook Academy to be a tuba player. (Even if it was just for a few weeks.) I liked that idea.

Not long after the band concert, Mommy and Seth invited Ms. Colman and Mr. Simmons over for supper again. It was Tuesday night. Andrew and I set the table. (I worked carefully. I did not break any plates.)

"What's for dinner?" I asked Mommy.

"Corn chowder, spinach pie, and vegetables," she replied.

"Yum," I said.

"Yuck," said Andrew. "Do I have to taste everything?"

"Yes," said Mommy. "But if you do not like something, you do not have to finish it. As long as you have tried it."

Seth came home at five-thirty. At six o'clock the doorbell rang.

"I'll get it!" I called.

I let Ms. Colman and Mr. Simmons in. At first, the adults just sat around in the living room and talked. Andrew wanted us to eat first, so he could get the tasting over with. But I wanted to listen to the grown-ups. They were talking about the wedding again.

"We have met with the caterer," said Ms. Colman. "This is the food we might serve at the reception. See what you think. Salmon rolls and tiny spinach quiches and cheese puffs. Those are the hors d'oeuvres."

"Yuck," said Andrew.

"For dinner — chicken kiev, vegetable mélange, and rice pilaf."

"Gross," said Andrew. "Do I have to taste everything at weddings, too?"

"And for dessert — cherries jubilee and, of course, the cake."

"Yummy," said Andrew, and Ms. Colman laughed.

"We have also talked to the florist," spoke up Mr. Simmons. "The flowers in the church will be asters and baby's breath."

"That sounds lovely," said Mommy.

"Speaking of flowers," said Ms. Colman. "Karen, Henry and I have something important to ask you. Would you like to be our flower girl?"

"You mean, be *in* the wedding?"

"Yes," said Ms. Colman. "I have a niece who is your age, and I had thought she might be our flower girl. But she will not be able to come to the wedding. My sister and her husband just live too far away. So Henry and I would be honored if you were our flower girl, Karen."

"Oh, thank you," I said softly. (I was even too excited to be noisy.) "I would love to be your flower girl."

I was the flower girl in Daddy's wedding, when he married Elizabeth. So I knew just what to expect. I would wear a beautiful dress, and carry beautiful flowers, and walk down the aisle of the church in front of Ms. Colman and Mr. Simmons.

I could not imagine anything lovelier. I decided I was the luckiest girl in the world.

Little Sister

Don't miss #38

KAREN'S BIG LIE

I moved on to the fourth problem: $9 + 8$ = _____ . I just could not answer that without counting on my fingers. I would *never* finish the quiz. I could not work fast enough.

I glanced over at Ricky's paper again. I bet his answers were almost all correct. I looked around for Ms. Colman. She was in the back of the room. She was busy with our workbooks. I looked back at Ricky's paper. He had moved on to the second column of problems.

And then I did something I knew I should not do. I began to copy Ricky's answers onto my paper.

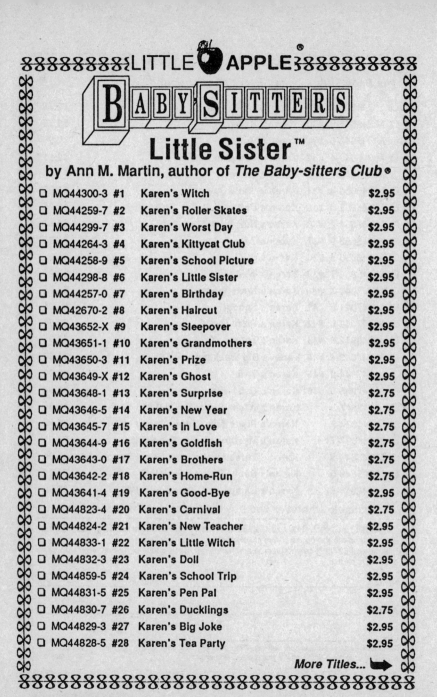

LITTLE ◉ APPLE ®

BABY-SITTERS
Little Sister ™

by Ann M. Martin, author of *The Baby-sitters Club* ®

More Titles... ➡